LEO and EMILY

OTHER YOUNG YEARLINGS YOU WILL ENJOY:

LEO and EMILY

by FRANZ BRANDENBERG

illustrated by ALIKI

A Young Yearling Book

Published by
Dell Publishing
a division of
Bantam Doubleday Dell Publishing Group, Inc.
666 Fifth Avenue
New York, New York 10103

The trademark Yearling® is registered in the U.S. Patent and Trademark
Office.

ISBN: 0-440-40294-8

Reprinted by arrangement with William Morrow & Company, Inc., on
behalf of Greenwillow Books

Printed in the United States of America

May 1990

10 9 8 7 6 5 4 3 2

W

for
Tabby
Millie
Tom

and
Fenella,
too

LEO and EMILY

CONTENTS

CHAPTER ONE
EARLY IN THE MORNING

"Leo!" called Emily.

Leo jumped out of bed.

"Leo, are you up?" called Emily.

"Shh!" said Leo.

"My parents

are still asleep."

"So are mine," said Emily.

"Can you come out?"

"I'll be right down,"

said Leo.

"If I turn on
   the light,
   my parents will wake up,"
   thought Leo. "I better
   get dressed in the dark."
   He took off his pajamas.
   He got his shirt and put it on.
   "That was easy," he said.

He got his trousers and put them on.

"That wasn't hard," he said.

He got his shoes and put them on.

"I got all dressed in the dark!" he said.

They won't believe it!

"Come on, Leo!" called Emily.

"I have something

very important to tell you."

"I am coming!" called Leo.

He ran out.

"What's the important news?"
he asked.
"Leo, I got all dressed
in the dark," said Emily.
"So did I!" said Leo.
"It shows," said Emily.

Look at your buttons!

"Your trousers are inside out.

You aren't wearing any socks,

and I bet you forgot

to put on your underwear."

"And you are wearing

your dress backward

and your shoes on the wrong feet,"

said Leo.

And your spaghetties
are untied!
HA HA HA

"What's going on so early?"
asked Leo's mother.
"It's still night,"
said Emily's father.

What's all the noise?

Who's out there?

HA HA

your spaghetties are untied! HA HA

13

"We got all dressed in the dark!"
said Leo and Emily.
"Without any help!"
said Emily's mother.

"They don't need us anymore,"
said Leo's father.
"Yes, we do," said Emily.
"But not as much," said Leo.

CHAPTER TWO

THE SWAP

1

"I wish I had your rabbit,"
said Emily.

"What will you give me for it?"
asked Leo.

"My tricycle," said Emily.

"I don't need another tricycle,"
said Leo.

"My ball," said Emily.

"I have a ball," said Leo.

"My encyclopedia," said Emily.

"You have to do better than that,"
said Leo.

"A wig," said Emily.

"It's a deal!" said Leo.

2

"Leo!" called Emily.

"What do you want so early
in the morning?" asked Leo.

"It's still dark."

"I have it," said Emily,
holding up a paper bag.

"I'll be right down," said Leo.

"Don't forget the rabbit,"
  said Emily.

"I won't," said Leo.

He took off his pajamas.

He put on his underpants,

his undershirt,

his shirt,

his trousers,

his socks and his shoes.

He got his flashlight
and the rabbit,
and ran outside.

"Did you get all dressed
   in the dark again?" asked Emily.
"Yes," said Leo.
"So did I," said Emily.
"This time I didn't forget anything,"
   said Leo.
"Your trousers are right-side-out,"
   said Emily.
"You are wearing your dress
   forward, and your shoes are
   on the right feet,"
   said Leo.

"Here is the wig," said Emily.

"And here is the rabbit," said Leo.

He shone his flashlight into the bag.
"Where did you get it?" he asked.
"It's my grandmother's," said Emily.
"Doesn't she need it?" asked Leo.
"She can do without it
for a day," said Emily.

"I thought it was mine
for keeps," said Leo.
"Perhaps you should just
borrow it," said Emily.
"I can't really give you
something that doesn't
belong to me."

All my life
I've waited
for a wig.

"The same with my rabbit," said Leo.

"It doesn't belong only to me.

It belongs to the whole family."

"Let's just lend them to each other

until tonight," said Emily.

"It's a deal!" said Leo.

3

"Where did you get the rabbit,

Emily?" asked her mother.

"And so early in the morning,"

said her father.

"Leo lent it to me

for the day," said Emily.

"That was nice of him,"

said her grandmother.

LOOK
LOOK
LOOK

29

"Breakfast is ready,"
  said Father.
"Please start without me,"
  said Grandmother.
"I have to find my wig.
  I must have misplaced it."
"I lent it to Leo for the day,"
  said Emily.
"I hope you don't mind."

"You traded it for the rabbit?"

asked Mother.

"You can't do that.

Grandmother needs her wig."

"I can do without it
for a day," said Grandmother.
"What on earth would Leo want
with a wig?" said Father.

4

Leo stood in front of his house,

holding the paper bag.

"Ten cents a peek!" he shouted.

All day long boys and girls,

and even some adults,

came to peek into the bag.

They giggled and shuddered.

Leo's wig-peek was

a great success.

He made

three dollars.

35

5

Emily, her parents,
and Grandmother
played with the rabbit all day.
"I haven't had so much fun
in a long time,"
said Grandmother.
When it was time
to return the rabbit,
she gave Emily three dollars.
"That's to buy your own rabbit,"
she said.

6

"Here is your grandmother's wig,"
  said Leo.
"Thank you for lending it to me."
"Here is your rabbit,"
  said Emily. "Thank you
  for letting me borrow it."
"And here are three dollars,"
  said Leo.
"That's to buy your own rabbit."
"Oh, thank you, Leo,"
  said Emily.

"Here are three dollars for you.

That's to buy your own wig."

"Thank you, Emily," said Leo.

"I think I'll get

a set of false teeth

and a top hat instead."

CHAPTER THREE
MAGIC

1

"Now that we have
a set of false teeth, a top hat,
and a rabbit, we can have
a magic show," said Emily.
"We have two rabbits," said Leo.
"That's even better," said Emily.

41

2

"Ladies and gentlemen," said Emily,
"may I present my assistant,
Abra Cadabra?"
She gave Leo a slap,
and his false teeth fell out.
The audience gasped.

"Don't worry," said Emily.

"They will grow back in."

Leo handed her the top hat.

"Now watch carefully!"

said Emily.

"One, two, three, hocus-pocus!"

She pulled her black rabbit

out of the hat.

"You put him in there,"

everyone shouted.

"That's no trick."

45

Emily put the rabbit
back into the hat.
"I shall do the trick again,"
she said.
"One, two, three, hocus-pocus!"
She pulled Leo's white rabbit
out of the hat.
"How did it change color?"
everyone asked.

"Now, Abra, let's see how your teeth
are coming along," said Emily.
"One, two, three, hocus-pocus!"

Leo smiled broadly.

"I told you they'd grow back in,"

said Emily.

"How did she do it?"

everyone asked.

"Magic!" said Leo.

The audience applauded.

Thank you, thank you.

BRAVO! Yea!

BRAVISSIMO

THREE CHEERS!

Congratulations to the rabbit, too!

3

"Leo!" called Emily.

"What do you want so late
at night?" asked Leo.
"It's already dark."

"I just wanted to tell you
something," said Emily.

"The magic show
    was a great success."
"Because of the rabbits,"
    said Leo.
"Because of your top hat
    and false teeth," said Emily.
"Because of your grandmother's wig,"
    said Leo.
"Because of both of you!"
    called Grandmother.

"Yes, because of us," said Emily.

"Because of all of us!" said Leo.

FRANZ and ALIKI BRANDENBERG are
husband and wife. They have collaborated on a
group of books about a family of cats–*A Secret
for Grandmother's Birthday*, *A Robber! A Robber!*,
I Wish I Was Sick, Too! and *A Picnic, Hurrah!*
–as well as on several books about a Fieldmouse
family, which include *What Can You Make of It?*,
Nice New Neighbors, *Six New Students*, *Everyone
Ready?* and *It's Not My Fault*. Among their
other collaborations are Jason and Alexa,
their two children.